My
Bus

Byron Barton

Greenwillow Books, *An Imprint of HarperCollinsPublishers*

My Bus. Copyright © 2014 by Byron Barton. All rights reserved. Printed in the United States of America. For information address HarperCollins Children's Books, a division of HarperCollins Publishers, 10 East 53rd Street, New York, NY 10022. www.harpercollinschildrens.com
The full-color art was created in Adobe Photoshop ™. The text type is ITC Avant Garde Gothic.
Library of Congress Cataloging-in-Publication Data: Barton, Byron, author, illustrator. My bus / Byron Barton. pages cm. "Greenwillow Books." Summary: "A bus driver named Joe heads out on his route, stopping at one bus stop after another to pick up passengers. He picks up five dogs and five cats in all, dropping nine of them off at the plane, train, or boat. The tenth passenger, a dog, Joe takes home"—Provided by publisher. ISBN 978-0-06-228736-6 (trade ed.)
(1. Buses—Fiction. 2. Transportation—Fiction. 3. Mathematics—Fiction. 4. Pets—Fiction.) I. Title. PZ7.B2848Mw 2014 (E)—dc23 2013007869
First Edition 14 15 16 17 LP/PX 10 9 8 7 6 5 4 3 2 Greenwillow Books

I am Joe.

This is my car.

This is my bus.

I drive my bus to town.

At my first stop,

one dog gets on my bus.

BUS
STOP

At my second stop,

two cats get on my bus.

At my third stop,

BUS
STOP

123 BUS

three cats get on my bus.

At my last stop,

four dogs get on my bus.

Five dogs and five cats

are on my bus.

I drive one dog and two cats

to the boat.

They sail away.

I drive two dogs and one cat

to the train.

They ride away.

I drive one dog and two cats

to the plane.

They fly away.

Cats and dogs sail,
ride, and fly away.

I park my bus. I get off.

One dog gets off.

I drive one dog home.

Meow.